# The Missing Horseshoe: A Christmas Mystery

## Sidney Sinclair Adventure #3

By Kathryn B. Butler

# Contents

# Chapter One

## A Christmas Party

Sidney Sinclair stared out the window at the falling snow. The flakes fluttered down lightly, some fast and some of them slow, but all of them melted immediately upon contact with the wet ground.

She sighed and pressed her face against the freezing glass.

"Stick!" she yelled.

She waited eagerly for snow every winter, but snow rarely stuck around in Tennessee. It was usually too warm. Sometimes, like now, the tiny flakes barely even touched the ground before disappearing. She watched hopefully, wishing with all her might that the ground would freeze so the snow would start to pile up. She would be disappointed if she didn't at least get enough snow out of this little storm to make a snowman.

"Sidney," her mother called from the kitchen. "It's almost time to go. Are you all packed up?"

"What do you think?" she shouted back with a grin, jumping up from her seat by the window. She had packed her overnight bag hours before and had everything she would need for Mrs. Fitzpatrick's sleepover in a neat pile by the front door.

Mrs. Fitzpatrick was the owner of Blue Moon Stables, a riding stable just across the road from Sidney's house, and she had decided to have a sleepover party to celebrate the holidays. Her riding students, Sidney included, had been looking forward to it for weeks, but Mrs. Fitzpatrick

1

refused to talk about the specifics of the party. She wanted everything to be a surprise, which made the students even more anxious for the big day to arrive.

Her mother appeared in the living room door, a wrapped plate in hand.

Sidney inhaled deeply. "Gingerbread?" she guessed.

Her mother smiled and nodded, her green eyes dancing. "Made especially for you."

Sidney licked her lips and held out her hands to take the plate, but Mrs. Sinclair grasped it tightly, holding it just out of her reach. "Not yet, Sid. We have to save some for the other party-goers."

"I'll just carry it," Sidney pleaded, tilting her head to look up at her mother as innocently as she could. Her mother narrowed her eyes, but gave the plate to Sidney. Its bottom felt warm against Sidney's hands.

"Mmm. Just out of the oven?"

"Yes, ma'am. And I better not catch you sneaking a bite." Mrs. Sinclair winked at Sidney and grabbed her goofy green Christmas sweater off the back of the couch.

"Don't worry," Sidney replied. "You won't catch me...." Sidney giggled and wiggled a finger under the aluminum foil wrapping covering the gingerbread. While her mother pulled the candy-cane-covered sweater over her head, mussing her ginger-colored hair, Sidney snapped off a tiny piece and popped it into her mouth. She tried to hold back the groan of pleasure.

"I hear munching," her mother said, glancing in the mirror by the front door. She straightened her hair and brushed the wrinkles out of the sweater with her hands. "How do I look?" She twirled for Sidney like a ballerina. Sidney swallowed her bite of gingerbread and licked the crumbs from her lips.

"Beautiful," Sidney said. And she meant it. Mrs. Sinclair always looked beautiful to Sidney, and she hoped to look just like her when she grew up. They already looked a lot alike, and Sidney's mother sometimes called Sidney "mini-me". The only big difference between the two was their eyes. Sidney's mother had sparkling green eyes, while Sidney had brown eyes, the same as her father.

"Let's go, then, Sid. I'm ready to eat some delicious holiday food. I hear Mrs. Fitzpatrick makes some killer hot chocolate," her mother said as she opened the front door, letting in a blast of cold air. Sidney shivered and stepped out into the wintry weather.

"Brrr. It's freezing out here. Let's hurry, Sid." Mrs. Sinclair slammed the front door behind them and locked it quickly then strode off toward the road.

Sidney tried to run ahead of her mother, but just breathing the icy air made her lungs ache. Slowing her steps, she stuck her tongue out, stretching it as far as it would go to try to catch a few snowflakes on her tongue. The delicate snow didn't taste at all, but she liked to feel the flakes melt and disappear in her mouth.

Mrs. Sinclair, who had Sidney's bags in tow, didn't notice Sidney lagging behind, so Sidney took the opportunity to sneak another bite of gingerbread.

"I wish Dad was here," Sidney said sadly, chewing on her bite of stolen cookie. Gingerbread reminded her of him. Her mother didn't like gingerbread, but her father did, and it was something they always shared during the holidays. He was the best at building gingerbread houses, and he always let Sidney decorate his masterpieces.

"He would be if he could, Sid. He'll be back tonight, though."

"Just not in time for the party?"

"Just not in time for the party," her mother repeated.

"He's never been out of town this close to Christmas before."

Mrs. Sinclair didn't respond. She just pursed her lips and continued walking.

Mr. Sinclair's job took him out of town often, but he usually reserved the week before Christmas and the week after just for family time. At first, Sidney hadn't believed him when he said he'd be leaving for a day or two, and that he'd miss Mrs. Fitzpatrick's Christmas party. It just wasn't like him.

*But he'll be back tonight,* Sidney thought, *and I'll see him first thing when I get home tomorrow morning. We'll make our gingerbread houses together.*

That's what he had promised Sidney before he left.

3

"I'm glad the stables are so close to home," Mrs. Sinclair said. "This snow just might start to stick after all. It's freezing out here."

The flakes stung Sidney's face and her bare hands, and the cold made her nose numb and red.

"I should've put my gloves on," Sidney said to her mother. Clinging to the plate of gingerbread with frozen fingers, she quickened her steps to catch up, and her mother glanced back, a worried look on her face.

Mrs. Fitzpatrick had told the riding students to bring their riding gear, but Sidney had decided to just wear hers instead. She had donned her warm winter jacket over an old flannel shirt and a worn pair of jeans. She had completed the ensemble with a beat-up pair of used cowboy boots she had picked up at the local tack shop. Her mother had protested against her outfit, but Sidney had insisted. She felt comfortable in her riding gear and that's what she wanted to wear. Besides, she had spiced it up a little bit, tying her red hair back with a green ribbon to add some Christmas cheer.

"Where are your gloves?" Her mother frowned.

"In my bag. Don't worry. I didn't forget them."

Mrs. Sinclair sighed. "You better not have."

Sidney knew her mother didn't want to return home to try to find them. Sidney's gloves never seemed to stay in a pair, and she was often sent to the barn wearing mismatching gloves because the true match couldn't be found. She had already lost two pairs of gloves completely and winter had barely started. Her sock situation wasn't much better, but at least if she *had* to wear one blue sock and one red one, her boots covered it up.

Sidney skipped past her mother and toward the large, lit up barn. "Almost there! Hurry up, Mom!"

A few cars were parked in the barn lot, and Sidney could hear voices inside.

She started to go toward the big barn doors, which led to the barn aisle and the stalls, but her mother stopped her.

"Not that way, Sid," she said quickly. "You know the party's being held in the new addition."

Mrs. Fitzpatrick called the new addition to the barn her "Christmas present to herself". It would be used for sleepovers and parties. The addition featured tables for crafting and games, two small rooms with bunk beds for sleeping, a small kitchen area, two bathrooms with several stalls and a shower a piece, and a small classroom complete with a whiteboard and desks. Sidney had walked through the new addition many times while it was in construction, but Mrs. Fitzpatrick had been keeping the area off limits while the final touches were added. This would be the first time Sidney would see it finished.

"I just wanted to say hello to Jasper and the others."

Her mother gestured toward the white door that led to the new addition. "Not now, Sid. Let's go into the party first and put the cookies down."

Sidney furrowed her brows. Mrs. Sinclair had a strange look on her face, and she didn't meet Sidney's questioning gaze.

"Don't you think it's more polite to say hello to the people first instead of the horses?" her mother continued, dropping Sidney's clothes bag so she could wipe snow from the shoulder of her sweater.

She didn't wait for Sidney to answer. Marching up to the door, she knocked carefully between the branches of a large prickly wreath. Sidney and Bryan, Mrs. Fitzpatrick's son, had decorated the wreath together only a few days earlier. Sidney had placed miniature plastic horses all around the perimeter, and Bryan had wrapped a red ribbon around the wreath, tying a big, pretty bow at the top.

The door opened and Mrs. Fitzpatrick beamed at her guests. "Come in, Sidney. Come in, Cara. I'm so glad you could make it. We've had several students call to say they weren't coming due to the snow. Even though it doesn't seem to be sticking."

Mrs. Sinclair gasped with relief as she stepped into the warmth of the barn addition.

"And poor Kelsey," Mrs. Fitzpatrick continued, "she was supposed to be here, but she traveled out of state to see family, and apparently it's a lot worse there. The snow is piling up, and she couldn't get a flight back."

"Kelsey won't be here?" Sidney frowned, disappointed. Kelsey was a junior riding instructor at Blue Moon Stables, and she had been Sidney's

5

camp counselor at Camp Sycamore Streams. She was a great rider and a good friend. Sidney had been looking forward to seeing her. Kelsey hadn't been giving as many lessons at Blue Moon Stables since school started. She would be applying to colleges soon and being a senior in high school was keeping her busy.

"Well, we're lucky in that regard," Mrs. Sinclair responded, "since we live just across the street. No trouble for us to get here."

"Yes, you and the Abbots," Mrs. Fitzpatrick said, gesturing for them to come in from the cold.

Sidney grabbed the bag her mother had dropped outside the door and followed her into the entryway.

"Speaking of the Abbots, is Jane here yet?" Sidney peered around the room as she peeled off her jacket and hung it on a peg by the door.

"Not yet, I'm afraid." Mrs. Fitzpatrick frowned, shaking her head, and her brown ponytail whipped back and forth. "Seems she's been delayed. Her mother called and said they should be here shortly, though."

Mrs. Abbot, Jane's mother, lived next door to Sidney and her family, and the Sinclairs knew the Abbots well.

"That's strange. She's never late to anything. Especially when it involves Christmas," Mrs. Sinclair said, concern in her green eyes. "She's always the first to arrive at these sort of things."

Mrs. Abbot celebrated the holidays like she did everything else: thoroughly and seriously. She threw parties, decorated extensively, and gave out gifts to everyone. If there was one time of year that Sidney liked and admired Mrs. Abbot, it was Christmastime.

"Well... I wouldn't worry. She'll be here soon enough." Sidney's riding instructor gave Mrs. Sinclair a look that Sidney understood. A look that said *I'll tell you later*, and Mrs. Sinclair nodded and let the matter drop.

"We were just about to dig in," Mrs. Fitzpatrick continued, leading the way into the big, open area where the crafting tables had been set up. Plates and trays brimming with food and drinks were displayed on every surface, both in the craft area and in the adjoining kitchen. Sausage balls, chips and dip, cookies, fruit, fancy sandwiches…. Sidney's eyes grew wide as she gazed at all the goodies.

Mrs. Fitzpatrick relieved her of the plate full of gingerbread, cramming it in between a white cake decorated with green and red sprinkles and a tray full of brownies.

"Are those your overnight clothes?" Mrs. Fitzpatrick gestured toward the bag Mrs. Sinclair still held.

"No, these are Sidney's games and books."

The riding instructor had advised the students to bring along games they thought would be fun to play in a group, and Sidney had brought along some books as well. She had gotten into the habit of reading at night before she fell asleep, and she was afraid she wouldn't be able to drift off without a book in her hands.

"I left my clothes bag by the door," Sidney said.

"Why don't you take your clothes into bunkroom two?" Mrs. Fitzpatrick fidgeted with the Christmas-themed cloth on the table, pulling it this way and that, careful not to knock off any food, until the edges were even. "I'll put the games with the others and introduce your mother to other students and their families. Everyone else is in the classroom. I put a Christmas movie on the TV in there, but it's almost over."

Sidney nodded and went to retrieve her overnight bag from the entryway. She hauled it into the second bunkroom, which was just off the kitchen, and dumped it on the nearest bed. The thick canvas felt a bit damp due to the melting snow, so she wiped her hands on her jeans and, on second thought, picked the bag up and dropped it beside the bed. She didn't want the sheets to get wet, and besides, she would have to wait for Jane to pick bunks. They always bunked together.

As she was standing there thinking, wondering when her friend would arrive, she heard something. Whispering. Coming from the kitchen. Peering around the doorway, Sidney held her breath. Her mother and Mrs. Fitzpatrick had already come back from putting away the other bag and had their heads together in the kitchen. They were speaking softly to one another while they uncovered the food.

"...she's ready...about time...responsible...I hope...."

Sidney didn't pay much attention to what they were saying until she heard her name. She just found it interesting that her mother and Mrs.

Fitzpatrick were whispering to one another and assumed it had to do with Mrs. Abbot not being there on time.

"Sidney... grown up so much... I'm afraid...."

Sidney narrowed her eyes at the pair. *What were they saying about her?* Sidney strained to make out their words, but she could only catch snippets of the conversation. Most of it was drowned out by the sound of crinkling foil and plastic as the covers were removed from all the plates and trays.

"...surprise...worried...."

That sounded like her mother. Sidney peered around the doorway. Part of her felt guilty about listening in, but a bigger part of her wanted to get closer and hear more. It sounded like a secret, and a juicy one. And it involved her, so why shouldn't she know?

She saw Mrs. Fitzpatrick shake her head while she leaned over the bowl of punch on the kitchen counter. "Definitely not..." The riding instructor set out paper cups by the bowl and put a large dipper into the red liquid. "She needs it..."

Mrs. Sinclair started to respond to whatever Mrs. Fitzpatrick had said, but she glanced toward the bunkroom and saw Sidney watching.

She snapped her mouth shut and pasted on a fake smile. "Sidney! Why don't you go tell everyone it's time to eat?"

Mrs. Fitzpatrick whirled around to stare at Sidney, too, her eyes wide. She quickly recovered and followed Mrs. Sinclair's lead with a cheery smile.

"Yep! Time to eat up! You can be our messenger."

Sidney just stared. She couldn't believe it. *She* had been caught eavesdropping, and her mother and Mrs. Fitzpatrick were the ones who seemed ashamed and embarrassed.

*They're definitely hiding something.*

"Go on, Sid." Her mother kept her eyes on the plate she was removing from the microwave. "This food will get cold again."

"What were you talking about?" Sidney asked.

Both women avoided her gaze.

8

"Nothing, Sid," Mrs. Sinclair said, and she fluttered her hands at her daughter as if to shoo her away. "Go."

Sidney smiled and tucked a strand of hair behind her ear, trying to suppress her excitement. She loved a good mystery, and this was certainly mysterious. She had never seen her mother act so peculiar.

"Of course," she said, "I'll be right back."

And she skipped off to make the announcement before her mother had time to realize she should be in trouble.

# Chapter Two

## Party Games

After eating until they could stuff themselves no more, the partygoers' parents began to trickle out into the cold. They would be back in the morning to pick up their children, but some of the little ones didn't seem to know that. For some, this was their first sleepover, and a few of the younger kids got teary-eyed. Mrs. Fitzpatrick intervened with games and distractions in those cases, and the moms and dads gave kisses, hugs, and reassurances and headed out into the snow, which had begun falling heavily.

Mrs. Sinclair was the last to leave. Before she left, she bent down and gave Sidney a swift peck on the cheek, whispering "I love you" in her ear. Sidney was sad to see her go. Not because she had never been to a sleepover before, but because she hadn't had a chance to figure out what her mother had been talking about with Mrs. Fitzpatrick, and she hadn't even thought of a good way to begin her investigation into the matter. How would she ever solve the mystery if her mother was gone?

Mrs. Sinclair opened the door and peered outside.

"It's getting colder out there all the time!" she exclaimed. She crossed her arms over her chest and glanced back at Sidney. "I think I even see a few flakes in the grass. We might have some snow on the ground in the morning."

Bryan came over to gaze past Mrs. Sinclair, his eyes wide. "Do you really think so?"

"I hope so, for your sake. See you tomorrow, Sid."

10

Mrs. Sinclair laughed and gave them one last wave before heading out into the thickly falling snow. Bryan took her place at the door, reaching a hand out to catch a few flakes.

"Can we turn on the news, Mom, and see what they're saying?" Bryan yelled back to Mrs. Fitzpatrick.

"If you shut that door you can," Mrs. Fitzpatrick shivered and gestured toward the classroom where the TV was set up, still running Christmas movies. "Don't let the cold air keep seeping in here."

Bryan slammed the door and raced off toward the classroom with Jimmy, a fellow riding student and another friend of Sidney's. Sidney had met both Jimmy and Bryan when she had started taking lessons at Blue Moon Stables the previous year. They had all taken classes together, and they had all spent the summer together at Camp Sycamore Streams, too.

Tonight, Jimmy had brought along his little brother for the sleepover. Jared had recently started taking lessons at Blue Moon Stables, and he liked to follow Jimmy around everywhere he went. He idolized his older brother, and copied him in both movement and dress. Jimmy had worn his usual jeans and a plaid, buttoned-down shirt with old, beat-up cowboy boots to the party. Similar to Sidney's outfit. Jared's outfit looked much the same, and he swaggered behind the two older boys into the classroom.

"Is Jane still coming, Mrs. Fitzpatrick?" Sidney was beginning to worry. It was five o'clock and very nearly dark outside. Everyone had already eaten and the games were about to begin.

"As far as I know," the riding instructor replied. She glanced up at the clock. "She should be here anytime now. In the meantime, we may have to get started without her."

At that moment, the door burst open, and Sidney's best friend, Jane Abbot, came in with a flurry of snow. Her cheeks were rosy with cold and her nose was as red as Rudolph's.

She tore off her mittens, gasping.

"There you are, Jane." Mrs. Fitzpatrick sighed. "I was beginning to wonder."

"Everything's ready," Jane said with a grin.

Mrs. Fitzpatrick nodded, a relieved expression on her face. Jane ran over to hug Sidney, her blue eyes dancing.

"What's ready?" Sidney asked. It seemed like every person at the party had something up his or her sleeve.

Jane put a finger to her lips and grabbed Sidney's hand, dragging her aside. "Mrs. Fitzpatrick has a surprise."

"Is that where you've been?"

Jane nodded, her short blonde hair bobbing up and down. "My mother's been helping arrange it, and I went with her."

Sidney squeezed Jane's cold hand. "Can you tell me?"

Jane opened her mouth to spill the beans but never got the chance. Mrs. Fitzpatrick clinked her glass of eggnog with a fork and all eyes turned toward her.

"Listen up, my young riders. It's time for the party games to begin! Abandon the board games for the moment."

"Party games?" the riding students whispered among themselves. A few of the younger kids ignored her and continued playing, but the older kids perked up.

"There will be prizes awarded for the winner of every game. And I have the ultimate prize for the winner of the most games." Mrs. Fitzpatrick held out a golden horseshoe. The letters CPGC had been painted across the top. "The winner of the most games will be crowned the Christmas Party Games Champion, and he or she will receive this horseshoe along with a gift card to Barney's Tack Shop."

"A real prize?" Jimmy cried out.

He stood up and crossed his arms. Bryan had sidled back in from the classroom and stood next to Sidney. He and Sidney exchanged glances. Jimmy was competitive, especially when it came to games, and he had a quick temper. He never backed down from a challenge, which Sidney admired, but he did get pretty upset when he lost.

Jimmy's little brother, who sat on the floor nearby, grinned up at him. "You'll win for sure, Jimmy."

"Don't be so sure, Jared." Jimmy glared around at all the other kids. "Looks like we've got some fierce competition."

When he said it, he smiled, but Sidney knew he was actually sizing up his competitors, and she rolled her eyes.

"What'd they say about the snow?" Sidney whispered.

Bryan's brown eyes gleamed. "It's starting to stick. They said an inch, maybe two, by morning."

Jane grabbed Sidney's arm and hopped up and down. "Snow! We can build a snowman, and we can go sledding, and have a snowball fight!"

Bryan smiled at Jane, reaching across Sidney to give her a one-armed hug.

"I'm glad you made it. Mom was worried you wouldn't. Is it ready?"

Mrs. Fitzpatrick shot a dark look in their direction and they fell silent. But as soon as she looked away, Jane nodded excitedly.

Mrs. Fitzpatrick continued holding the horseshoe for all of them to see. A few kids even got up from their seats to get a closer look at it.

"So, are you ready to compete for this?"

Mary, a new student at the stables, sneered at the award.

"I wouldn't mind the gift card. I could use it to buy Sadie a new halter, but that horseshoe's nothing special. It's just a regular old horseshoe with gold paint and letters on it."

Mrs. Fitzpatrick pretended not to hear her, and Sidney felt her blood begin to boil. Mary had only been riding at Blue Moon Stables for a few weeks, and Sidney was struggling to like her. When Sidney had first met Bryan, she had gotten a bad first impression. However, in the end he had turned out to be a great friend, so she wanted to give Mary a chance. The new girl seemed determined to ruin everyone's fun all the time, though. She constantly criticized the other riders and their horses, and frequently bragged about all the ribbons she had won with her beautiful Quarter Horse, Sadie, at local shows.

Sadie was an expensive show horse and nothing like the lesson horses at Blue Moon Stables. Sidney didn't think that made her more important or more special than the other horses at the barn, but Mary seemed to think it did.

Sadie boarded at Blue Moon Stables, and Mary and her father, Mr. Wright, had given Mrs. Fitzpatrick specific instructions for her care, including a note that asked no one else to touch her. So Sidney and Bryan, who both worked in the stables, were asked not to handle Sadie, and Mrs. Fitzpatrick had to care for Sadie all on her own.

"I think the prize is great." Jimmy narrowed his blue eyes at Mary, his shoulders hunched forward angrily. He'd had more trouble with Mary than the rest of them. He couldn't help but respond to her rude comments, and it often got him into trouble with Mrs. Fitzpatrick, who seemed reluctant to scold Mary.

Mary shrugged her petite shoulders and lowered her eyes, backing away from the group surrounding Mrs. Fitzpatrick.

"Anyway," the riding instructor said, giving Jimmy a disapproving look, "we should get started now. The first game will be pin-the-tail-on-Jasper!"

Jane grabbed Sidney's hand and pulled her forward to get in line. A blown up photograph of Sidney's favorite lesson horse, Jasper, hung on the wall behind one of the craft tables. Mrs. Fitzpatrick handed the first student in line a fake horsetail with a pushpin attached to it and a blindfold. "Let the games begin!"

***

Somehow, Mary ended up winning not just the first game, but the second as well. And the third game, musical chairs, didn't end well for the other students either.

"Cheater!" Jimmy called out when Mary slipped past him and into the last chair. There was no way he could get to the chair without knocking her down.

"She didn't cheat, Jimmy," Mrs. Fitzpatrick said sternly. "That isn't very nice. She got to the chair first."

"You were just too slow." Mary stuck out her tongue at Jimmy behind Mrs. Fitzpatrick's back, but the riding instructor turned just in time to see it.

14

"That's not nice either, Mary," Mrs. Fitzpatrick said. "I won't have that behavior from either of you."

Mary shrugged and crossed her arms while Mrs. Fitzpatrick retrieved the prize for the musical chairs game, a small glass figurine of a horse and rider, and presented it to Mary.

"That's beautiful," Jane gushed, running over to get a closer look. The delicate glass horse had its front hoof lifted and its head thrown back with its mane blowing in the wind. The rider looked off into the distance with one hand shielding his eyes from the sun. "They look like explorers."

Mary clutched it close to her chest, away from Jane's gaze. "Can we play the next game now?"

Mrs. Fitzpatrick sighed, glancing around at the disgruntled students. Mary winning three games in a row hadn't gone over well.

"Let's take a quick break while I do the evening feedings in the barn. Everyone can get a drink and a snack and then we'll finish up the games. How does that sound?"

Jimmy grumbled, brushing a hand through his messy blond hair.

"I think we should just get it over with. It's obviously rigged," he muttered as he stomped off toward the refrigerator.

Bryan gave Sidney a fleeting look of frustration and followed close behind him.

"I'll cheer him up," he promised as he passed Mrs. Fitzpatrick.

"And I'll help you feed the horses," Sidney piped up.

But Mrs. Fitzpatrick shook her head.

"Not tonight, Sidney. I want you to enjoy the party, and that means you are absolutely forbidden to be in the barn. Stay in here and have fun with your friends. I'll be back in a few minutes and we can get the games going again."

Sidney started to argue, but Mrs. Fitzpatrick gave her a look that Sidney knew meant business, so she shut her mouth and turned to Jane instead.

"Let's pick bunks. I was waiting for you."

15

She hadn't had a chance to tell her about the snippets of conversation she had overheard between her mother and Mrs. Fitzpatrick, and she wanted to do so in private.

***

"It has to be about a Christmas present, right?" Jane said quietly, stowing Sidney's bags under the bunk they had chosen to share. "I overheard my mom telling my dad that she bought me a new sweater and new riding boots for Christmas just last week. I didn't want to ruin it, so I acted like I didn't hear anything. I'll have to pretend to be surprised when I open them."

"New riding boots?" Sidney giggled and plopped down on the bed. "You just got a new pair a few months ago. Does your mom think you need new boots every time you get manure or mud on them?"

Jane rolled her blue eyes skyward and frowned. "Pretty much. You know Mom. But back to your problem…."

"What do you think it is? And why would she be worried about it?" Sidney frowned. "I just can't think of anything to explain it, and it's scaring me."

Jane tapped her finger on her chin. "I don't know. It is odd, Sid, but you'll find out soon enough if it's something to do with Christmas. It's only a week away."

"Maybe-" Sidney started, but she never got to finish her thought. Mary burst into the room, tears streaming down her face.

"Sidney?" Mary sniffled as she brushed wisps of raven-colored hair from her wet cheeks. "Mrs. Fitzpatrick says she needs you."

Sidney stood up quickly from the bunk. "What's wrong?"

Mary took a deep, rattling breath. "It's Sadie. I think she's sick."

# Chapter Three

## Sadie's Bellyache

Sidney and Jane followed Mary from the bunkroom and back into the party area. The other kids seemed unfazed. Some of them munched on snacks and sipped from plastic cups, while others sat on the floor or at the craft tables finishing the board games they had abandoned when the party games began.

Mary sobbed softly while she led the girls across the room and to the door that separated the new addition from the actual barn. She glanced back as her hand touched the knob.

"No one else is supposed to go in," she said to Jane. "Some sort of surprise."

Jane reached out and put a comforting hand on the girl's arm.

"I know about the surprise, but I'll wait here and make sure no else bothers you."

Mary shrugged Jane's hand away and nodded, tears still spilling from her troubled green eyes. She struggled between emotions, seeming angry, sad, and grateful all at the same time

"Let's go," Sidney said, giving Mary a nudge. She didn't want her to break down in front of everyone. It would be embarrassing for her and upsetting for everyone else. Sidney's heart rate increased as the two girls slipped through the door quietly, leaving Jane to stand guard inside.

The door opened into a small barn office Mrs. Fitzpatrick had fashioned from one of the stalls. The new wooden floors gleamed, but the

17

beat-up wooden desk in the corner was already worn and well-used. Sidney knew that was where Mrs. Fitzpatrick stored all her files on the horses. She gave the room a quick once over. A new phone had been installed. It hadn't been there the last time Sidney had been in the office. It was on the desk amid an assortment of papers and documents that looked like they were waiting to be sorted and filed.

"Through here," Mary said, leading the way through the office door and into barn aisle.

The freezing air hit Sidney, taking her breath away, and she shivered. She had grabbed her coat, but it just wasn't thick enough to keep out the cold. The barn doors were closed, but she could still feel a breeze from somewhere. *The wind must be picking up out there.*

"And there's the surprise." Sidney stopped short right outside the office door. "How did they get that thing in here without anyone seeing?"

A large red sleigh took up much of the barn aisle. It had been decorated for Christmas with shiny brass bells and brightly colored tinsel. *Like Santa's sleigh.* There was something different about this sleigh, though. Instead of the snow runners often seen on sleighs, this one had wheels so it could be used even when there wasn't any snow. Sidney knew it wasn't really Santa's sleigh, but she couldn't take her eyes off of it. It looked magical somehow in the dim light of the barn.

Mary barely glanced at it before hurrying off toward Sadie's stall. She stopped impatiently to tap her foot on the ground and gesture for Sidney to follow when she realized she wasn't behind her.

"Come on," she hissed, tossing her head. "Mrs. Fitzpatrick's waiting."

Sidney ripped her gaze away from the sleigh, and trotted down the barn aisle toward Mary reluctantly. She usually liked the nighttime noises of the stables, but tonight the peaceful sound of the horses tearing hay from their mangers and chewing contentedly had been replaced with restless movements and agitation. Jasper, the big black gelding she usually rode during lessons, stuck his head over the top of his stall door as she passed and bumped her arm with his nose. She stopped long enough to pat the horse affectionately, and he whinnied softly, his nostrils fluttering beneath her gloved hand.

"It's okay, boy," she whispered. "It's nothing to worry about."

18

Mary reached Sadie's stall and peered over the door, a worried look on her face. Sidney heard a groan from inside.

Mary motioned for her to hurry, and Mrs. Fitzpatrick's came into view over the stall door as she popped up from where she must have been kneeling.

"Oh, good, Sidney," she said. "I need your help."

"What do you want me to do, Mrs. Fitzpatrick?"

"I have to stay with Sadie. I've called the Wright's vet, but he doesn't know when he'll be able to get here. He's got other cases and the snow is really slowing things down. I need someone to get on the phone with all the vets in the area. This is an emergency. We need a vet here right away. Call every vet close by."

"But, Mrs. Fitzpatrick, Dr. Teller is the best. That's why my father chose him as Sadie's vet." Mary clenched the stall door so hard her knuckles turned white. The tears still streamed down her face, but she didn't seem to notice.

"I know that, Mary, but Dr. Teller may not be able to make it in time. We need someone here as soon as possible, and he's on the other side of town, in the snow, with another patient."

"But…" Mary's voice trailed off and she looked on the verge of collapse. Sidney had never seen anyone so upset. She grabbed Mary by the hand. She could feel how cold the girl's skin was even through her gloves.

"Come on, Mary. Help me in the office. You can look up the veterinarians' numbers for me while I call them."

Mrs. Fitzpatrick nodded gratefully, but she still looked worried. "By the way, Sidney, have you seen Bryan and Jimmy?"

Sidney shook her head. "Bryan said he was going to cheer Jimmy up. That's the last time I saw them. Maybe they went out in the snow."

Mrs. Fitzpatrick shrugged and gave a frustrated sigh. "I could really use his help right now. Is there someone responsible keeping an eye on the kids? I meant for him to do it."

"Jane's in there, Mrs. Fitzpatrick. She won't let the younger ones do anything dangerous."

"Good." Mrs. Fitzpatrick turned back to her charge.

19

Sidney glimpsed the horse for the first time, and what she saw made her stomach clench. Sadie was down on the floor of her stall. Wood shavings clung to the horse's chest and sides, sticking to her sweat-covered body. The usually stoic, quiet horse appeared to be sweating profusely despite the freezing temperatures, and she had a pained look in her eyes.

Sidney turned Mary away from the scene and led her back to the office. She pushed the office door shut behind them, shutting out the cold, and removed her jacket. She handed it Mary.

"Wipe those tears away before they freeze on your face. We need to get to work. Sit here," Sidney pulled out the desk chair, "and look through this for local vets. Start making a list of the closest ones."

Sidney rifled through the drawers until she found a phone book and plopped it down on the desk in front of the girl.

"And I'll use this emergency list. Thank goodness Mrs. Fitzpatrick is always prepared."

A list of emergency numbers was taped to the desk beside the phone, and Sidney glanced over it quickly. Three veterinarians were listed along with the contact information for a farrier and a few emergency numbers in case of a fire or a student injury.

Dr. Teller was the first name on the contact sheet, but Sidney knew he had already been called, so she skipped his name and went on to the next one.

Mary watched her face closely as she called the first vet. Sidney explained the situation to the person on the other end of the phone, listened for a moment, then shook her head. Mary looked back down at the phone book, crestfallen. The next call was the same. It was a busy, and nasty, night. The weather wasn't on their side.

Sidney sighed. "Next number."

"This isn't working." Mary scrunched up her face, which was already swollen from crying, to try to keep the flow of tears at bay. "No one's going to come."

"Someone's going to come." Sidney clenched her teeth together. "Give me a number from the phone book."

Mary rattled off a number. "His office is on the other side of town."

20

Sidney dialed as fast as she could. She listened to the rings while she rubbed Mary's shoulder reassuringly.

"Dr. Parson's office."

Sidney took a deep breath and launched into an explanation of their problem for the third time. The lady on the other end of the line listened politely, asking questions when appropriate.

"We need someone here now," Sidney said finally. "It's really bad."

"I understand. Dr. Parsons is out on a call right now. Let me give him a ring on his cell and I'll call you right back, sweetie."

"Okay," Sidney said. "Thank you so much."

"Just a minute." The line went dead, and Sidney set the phone down.

"She's going to get in touch with him. He's out on a call."

The door to the new addition opened and Jane stuck her head in. She looked surprised to see them sitting at the desk. "What's going on?" she said, trying to keep her voice low.

Sidney updated her as quickly as she could, all the while staring at the phone, willing it to ring.

Jane nodded curtly when she finished. "I'll keep an eye on the kids. You just get a vet to Sadie."

Jane pulled the door shut to get back to the younger children.

*Brrrng. Brrrng.*

Sidney had the phone up to her ear in a flash, before the second ring had even finished.

"Is he coming?" she blurted out.

The woman on the other end laughed softly. "You're in luck. He just finished up with another patient and he happens to be close by. I gave him the address. He should be there in about ten minutes."

Sidney's heart soared and she patted Mary on the back smiling widely.

"Thank you!" she exclaimed to the woman. "And Merry Christmas!"

21

"Merry Christmas to you, too," the woman replied. "I hope everything turns out okay."

Sidney hung up the phone and skipped off to tell Mrs. Fitzpatrick the good news. Then she went outside to wait on the vet. Mary went with her. She couldn't bear to stay with Mrs. Fitzpatrick and Sadie, and Sidney didn't think it was a good idea for her to stay with them anyway. Her anxiety only made matters worse.

For the first time, Sidney felt a little uncomfortable with the girl. They had never been alone before or had a real conversation. Mary's snippy attitude had turned Sidney off from the beginning, so it had been difficult to even carry on small talk at the barn.

"You seem really close to Sadie," Sidney said to fill the quiet. The snow had indeed begun to stick, and big, fat snowflakes fell heavily from the sky. It seemed to muffle out all the noise. "How long have you had her?"

Mary sniffled and rubbed her nose.

"A long time." She hesitated and glanced sideways at Sidney. "My mother gave her to me."

"Really? I've never met her. Your father always brings you to lessons, right?"

Mary's jaw clenched. "Yes. You won't be meeting her. She died when I was eight."

Sidney almost gasped, but she held it in.

"Oh, I'm so sorry. I had no idea."

Mary shrugged and looked away, but Sidney didn't see any tears. *She's probably used them all up.*

"I usually don't bring it up. People act weird when they know."

It was true. Sidney didn't know what to say. Just imagining losing her own mother brought tears to her eyes and made her feel numb all over. Plus, she felt embarrassed that she hadn't known. She should have been more sensitive.

Sidney put an arm around Mary's shoulder. This time, the girl made no move to shrug it off or turn away like she had from Jane.

"I'm sure Sadie will be fine."

"I hope so," Mary said. "She was the last present Mom gave me, and the best. She gave her to me for my eighth birthday. Dad didn't want to buy me a horse, but Mom insisted. She said I deserved one after working so hard."

This information spilled out of her quickly, like she'd been holding it in for a long time.

"I've had her for three years now."

They fell silent, watching the snow.

"I think it's going to be more than an inch or two," Sidney said.

She brushed snow from her shoulders and shook her head to get it out of her hair. A fine dusting had already covered Mary's ebony locks, and snow clung to her fuzzy green sweater all over, making it appear mottled in color.

"You're really good at the games. How do you keep winning?"

"Just luck, I guess." Mary gave Sidney a small smile.

"Well, just wait until this summer. Mrs. Fitzpatrick told me she is going to add horseback games to the lessons. Kind of the like the games they play in a gymkhana. You would be awesome at that."

Mary nodded enthusiastically.

"They used to have those competitions at my old barn. Timed games on horseback and races and stuff. They were a lot of fun." She paused and rubbed her nose again. It had turned bright red in the cold. "Sadie always loved competing."

"Well, you should talk to Mrs. Fitzpatrick about it." Sidney tried to keep her tone light. "Maybe she would even have a show here at Blue Moon Stables."

"That's a good idea. There's the vet, I think." Mary pointed. Two beams of light shone through the snow and illuminated the road in front of Blue Moon Stables, revealing a thin sheet of white on the black asphalt. *The roads are getting bad. It's a good thing he was so close.*

The driver turned cautiously into the driveway and killed the engine, walking up the hill on foot.

23

"Easier just to park down there, I think," he said when he got up to the barn, a bag filled with medicines and veterinary tools on his arm. He wore thick coveralls and heavy boots covered with mud, and he had a sandy-colored beard that almost looked white with snow. He looked cold and tired, but he smiled kindly at the two girls. Sidney let out a breath and smiled back. His presence was reassuring.

"The patient's this way," Sidney said.

She led the vet into the barn, glad to have her part of the job finished. Mary followed close behind the pair.

"Would you like a drink or anything?" Sidney asked as an afterthought. The man looked practically frozen.

*And he'll probably be out in this weather for a while yet. Sadie's probably not his last patient of the night.*

"That would be nice. If you've got anything hot."

"Mrs. Fitzpatrick makes the best hot chocolate." Sidney smiled at the older man. "I'll put in extra marshmallows."

He grinned and pulled his hat down lower over his ears. "Perfect. It's nippy out tonight. Why don't you girls get us all a cup and I'll take care of this horse. What's the patient's name?"

Mary took a deep breath, and reached for Sidney's hand. "Sadie. Her name's Sadie."

# Chapter Four

## Stolen Prizes

When Sidney and Mary re-entered the party, chaos had ensued. Jane still stood guarding the door, her blue eyes wide.

"What's going on?" Sidney asked as one of the younger kids, a child she had never seen before, raced past her, barely avoiding a collision.

Another small kid, who seemed to have been chasing the first, slid to a halt right in front of Sidney and grinned at her, his face smeared with white frosting and chocolate.

"Tag! You're it!" he yelled and slapped a sticky hand into her stomach before taking off again.

"Oof!" Sidney leaned over.

"I think he wants you to chase him, Sid." Jane giggled. The wild little boy stopped about ten feet away and danced on the spot, sticking his tongue out at Sidney.

Sidney rubbed the spot where the kid had smacked her and made a face right back at him.

"This is exactly why I don't help with the younger kids' lessons. They're crazy."

"I think they're just getting restless. And they're eating too many sweets." Jane gestured at the massacred dessert table. "Don't worry, though. I haven't let them do anything dangerous. How's Sadie?"

"Well, the vet's here. So, hopefully, she'll be okay. Mrs. Fitzpatrick has to stay out there and help him, though. We came in to get some hot chocolate."

"I'll help you make it."

Mary excused herself to the bathroom to clean up her tear-swollen face while the other girls went to the kitchen area to heat up some water.

Sidney had just poured the steaming water into two cups filled with Mrs. Fitzpatrick's special hot chocolate mix when she heard a yell. She set the pan down quickly, her hands shaking, and whirled around. But before she could say anything, Jane took charge.

"What is going on?" Jane demanded, in as threatening a voice as she could. "Who yelled?"

Everyone froze. For the first time, the party fell totally silent. All the other riding students stared at Jane, surprised.

"I'm serious," Jane continued. "I want to know who yelled right this second."

A little girl with long blonde braids held up her hand hesitantly. Her bottom lip trembled.

"It was you?" Jane said in a kinder voice.

The girl shook her head and pointed. At Jared, Jimmy's little brother.

Jared's face went pale, but he didn't deny it.

"Why did you do that, Jared? You scared us."

"I can't find my brother. Derek said he left me here." Jared pointed at the boy sitting next to him, a short, mean little boy whom Sidney had the misfortune of knowing somewhat well. He attended riding lessons twice a week, and his mother sometimes left him at the barn for hours after his lesson instead of picking him up right away. Sidney felt sorry for the boy. She knew he hated being left at the barn, but he could be a real pain. He liked to play tricks on her if she happened to be at the stables and would follow her around making fun of her and laughing at everything she did. Derek held his hands up in the air innocently.

"Well, he did, didn't he? He's not here."

26

Jane glanced at Sidney, and Sidney shook her head. She had no idea where Jimmy had gotten to.

"Your brother didn't leave you, Jared," Jane reassured him. "I don't know where he is, but he's here somewhere. So is Bryan. They just went off somewhere together. Come over here with us." She held out a hand and Jared trotted over. "We'll make you a cup of hot chocolate."

Jared smiled reluctantly and grasped Jane's fingers.

"I know why they ran off!" Derek said suddenly, a malicious grin on his face. He pointed to the place on the table where Mrs. Fitzpatrick had piled the prizes for the party games. "The horseshoe is gone. So is the gift card. The prizes have been stolen!"

This time Sidney stopped the uproar. She quieted the muttering group with an upraised hand, thinking Derek was just trying to cause trouble, but when she looked at the table, she saw he was right. The horseshoe and the envelope containing the gift card had been removed from the table.

"This isn't funny. Where are the prizes?" Sidney crossed her arms and glared at the gathered children in turn, but no one answered.

*** 

Sidney handed Mrs. Fitzpatrick a warm mug of steaming cocoa and patted her arm. She looked exhausted. Slight wrinkles had begun to show around her brown eyes, and her mouth drooped uncharacteristically. Her brown ponytail even seemed limp.

"Well, things didn't go as planned tonight, did they?" she said with a laugh.

Sidney smiled sadly and shook her head. "I'm sorry, Mrs. Fitzpatrick. I know you spent a lot of time planning this party."

"We can always have another party. I just hope Sadie will be okay."

Sidney agreed quietly. She couldn't forget what Mary had told her out in the snow. Sadie was a special horse, and she meant so much to Mary.

27

Sidney watched as the kids ransacked the kitchen. She had updated Mrs. Fitzpatrick on the situation with the missing prizes, and Mrs. Fitzpatrick had been disappointed to say the least. She had sent Jane off in search of Bryan and Jimmy, and she'd had the kids clean up the mess they had made of the area and search for the missing horseshoe and gift card at the same time.

"No luck," Mary said, brushing a strand of black hair from her eyes. She had calmed down after the vet arrived and ceased her crying, but the tenseness in her shoulders and the terseness of her voice gave her worry away. Sadie wasn't out of the woods yet, and Mary wouldn't fully relax until she knew her horse was safe.

Mrs. Fitzpatrick shook her head. "It really was just a horseshoe, Mary. Like you said. Don't worry about it."

"Oh, but I didn't mean it, Mrs. Fitzpatrick. You know that."

The riding instructor put an arm around Mary's shoulders. "I called your dad about Sadie."

Mary looked up hopefully. "Is he coming?"

"He said he'd wait until morning. The snow is just too much tonight. It's worse than everyone thought it would be."

"I think we're going to get a lot," Mary agreed.

The front door banged open and snow whirled in, the flakes blowing about the room on a blast of freezing air. Jane ran in, hugging herself to keep warm, and Bryan and Jimmy followed her. Neither one would meet Mrs. Fitzpatrick's eye.

"Sorry, Mom," Bryan said. "We didn't realize anyone was looking for us."

"We'll talk about that later, Bryan," she replied sternly. "Right now we need your help looking for our missing prizes. Did Jane tell you?"

Bryan nodded and snow showered from his shaggy brown hair onto the floor, quickly melting to form small puddles around his sneakers.

Jimmy glared at Mary. "Maybe she took it."

Mary rolled her eyes. "Why would I take it? I was already going to win it anyway."

28

Sidney snorted, trying to hold in her laughter, and Jimmy turned his angry gaze on her.

"Be nice, Jimmy," she said. She was used to his temper and competitive spirit, but she knew he was a big softie at heart. "Do you know about Sadie?"

Jimmy shrugged and looked away.

"Yeah. I'm sorry about your horse, Mary. I hope she'll be okay."

An uncomfortable silence settled on the group, and Mrs. Fitzpatrick smiled.

"We can get along, guys. We all have something in common. Our horses. And we all love Blue Moon Stables, right? You all like your riding instructor?" She winked and grinned at Jimmy.

"We do *most* of the time," he responded with a teasing grin.

Everyone smiled.

"We all love Christmas, and the snow," the riding instructor continued. "And we all want to have a good time tonight, don't we?"

The students nodded.

"Good. Can you help me to make that happen?"

The group nodded again.

"Then let's forget about the prizes for now. I can always get another prize. It doesn't have to be given out tonight." She clasped her hands in front of her and beamed. "Let's go Christmas caroling!"

"Can we take the sleigh like we planned?" Jane asked.

"What sleigh?" Jimmy's eyes got wide, but Mrs. Fitzpatrick shook her head.

"I'm afraid not. The roads are getting too bad. It's on wheels, remember, because we didn't know it would actually snow. We'll have to do it the old-fashioned way."

"Sleighs are pretty old-fashioned." Jimmy put his hands on his hips. "Nobody uses them anymore."

"Well, even more old-fashioned. We're going to be walking. Help me organize the kids. I have candles for us to carry. And we can go sing Christmas carols."

"At my house?" Sidney asked excitedly. "And Jane's?"

Mrs. Fitzpatrick nodded. "And the rest of the neighborhood."

\*\*\*

"We're terrible at this, but I don't even care," Jimmy said as they traipsed from Jane's front yard to the Sinclairs' front yard. Sidney could see the Christmas tree she and her mother had put up weeks before gleaming in the porch window. With the snow swirling in front of the cozy little house and the smoke seeping out of the chimney, it looked like a picture from a Christmas card. As Sidney admired the pretty scene, her father's face appeared in the top pane of the window.

"Hey, Dad," Sidney called, waving for him to come out. He gave her a big smile and disappeared. The front door opened a moment later and both of Sidney's parents came out onto the porch, wrapping themselves up in their coats.

"He made it back from his trip safe and sound," Sidney said to Jane with satisfaction.

Mr. Sinclair put an arm around Mrs. Sinclair's waist. He looked excited and happy, and the pair glanced at each other and smiled secretively. *Something's up and he knows about it, too.* Sidney narrowed her eyes at her parents and elbowed Jane, but before she could voice her thoughts to her best friend, Mrs. Fitzpatrick took her place in front of the group and waved a riding crop like a conductor's stick to get their attention.

"Ready? Silent Night!"

The carolers launched into the song, some starting too early, some too late, and many of them off key, but it sounded magical to Sidney. She quickly forgot her worries about her parent's surprise, and gave her full energy to the song.

At one point, she glanced over at Jimmy. He had his hand on Jared's shoulder, and Jared was looking up at him with shining eyes.

When the group paused for a breath between songs, Sidney pointed the sweet scene out to Jane.

"Jared just worships him," Sidney said. "Isn't it cute?"

Jane grasped Sidney's gloved hand and gave it a squeeze.

"He's adorable. I wish Jimmy would pay more attention to him, though. He tries awfully hard to impress him."

Sidney agreed quietly. Jimmy wasn't always sensitive to other people's feelings, and he seemed totally unaware of his brother's admiration.

"I would offer you hot chocolate," Sidney's mother called to the carolers, "but after having Mrs. Fitzpatrick's, it would taste terrible, and I'm sure this group has had plenty of sweets already."

"You have no idea," Mrs. Fitzpatrick said loudly, shaking her head. She had cheered up considerably since they had started caroling. She and Mary had left their troubles at the barn with Dr. Parsons. At first, Mary had insisted on staying with her horse, but the vet had assured Mary he'd be with Sadie until they returned, which wouldn't be long.

The carolers laughed and, led by Mrs. Fitzpatrick, continued on their way. Sidney's parents gave her a final wave and watched as she followed the group toward the next house, about a half a mile down the road.

"Caroling was a good idea," Mr. Sinclair said, watching the kids trail off. "They're going to be exhausted by the time they get back. After traipsing through the snow, they'll probably fall right into bed."

Mrs. Sinclair laughed and put an arm around her husband's shoulder.

"Do you think Sidney's guessed? She overheard something, but I couldn't tell how much."

He shook his head. "She would've said something if she knew. You know how she is. I think she'll be good and surprised."

Mrs. Sinclair shivered, more from excitement than the cold.

"I can't wait. This is the most excited I've been for Christmas in a long time."

31

"I know what you mean." Sidney's father looked up at the snow. The flakes danced playfully in the soft glow of the porch light. "There's something different about this year. It feels like there's a bit of magic in the air."

The pair retreated into the warmth of the Sinclair home, and the Christmas carolers trudged off to spread their Christmas cheer, none of them aware that just across the road, up in the barn, something magical was indeed happening at that very moment.

# Chapter Five

## A Discovery

Sidney flopped down onto the bunk and snuggled into the Western-style comforter, wrapping the blanket snugly around her frozen feet.

"Oh, it feels like *heaven*." Sidney groaned, wiggling her thawing toes. A warm, comfortable glow washed over her, and her eyes felt suddenly heavy.

Jane climbed the little ladder to the top bunk. The bed squeaked as she burrowed under the covers over Sidney's head.

"Night, Sid," she whispered.

"Night, Jane," Sidney whispered back.

Sidney's father had been right. The long walk through the cold and snow had exhausted the group. Sidney could already hear a chorus of snores around her and the lights hadn't even been turned out yet.

Mary was the only one who didn't look tired. She just looked miserable. When the group had made it back to the barn, the vet had refused to let her see Sadie. He even had the nerve to grin at her when she complained.

"Just a few more minutes," he had said, and he had laughed.

"How could he laugh?" Mary said to Sidney. It was the fourth or fifth time she had said it.

Sidney sighed. Mary had chosen the bunk right across from she and Jane's, and instead of lying down to go to sleep like everyone else, she sat with her knees drawn up to her chin. It looked like the tears were about to begin again so Sidney edged out from under her warm covers reluctantly and went to sit beside her.

"I'm sure it's because he knows she'll be fine," Sidney said.

Jane peered over the top of the bunk. "You should just go to sleep, Mary. When you wake up, she'll be better."

Sidney nodded and picked up Mary's pillow to force it into her hands. "Sleep. Staying up all night won't help anything. Besides, Mrs. Fitzpatrick promised to come get you, whether you're asleep or not, once the vet leaves."

Mary accepted the pillow, but her eyes weren't on Sidney, they were on the place where her pillow had been.

"Where did those come from?" Mary said, her voice shaking. "I didn't put them there."

Sidney turned back, and she stared, too. A shiny golden horseshoe, the missing prize, and the gift card lay in the place where Mary's pillow had been.

"Someone hid them under my pillow," Mary said, confused.

Sidney didn't say anything. She was just beginning to like Mary. Could she believe her? Why would anyone hide the prizes under *her* pillow?

Jane clambered down from her bunk. She tried to hide the prizes again before anyone could see, but one of the other girls had already spotted them.

"She stole the prizes!" The girl yelled, pointing at Mary. "They found them. It was her! We should go tell Mrs. Fitzpatrick."

Jane tried to shush the girl, but she wasn't having it. She leapt from her bed and raced away to get Mrs. Fitzpatrick. Another girl followed and the rest looked up sleepily from their bunks. Some interested, some annoyed.

Mary looked to Sidney and Jane desperately.

"You believe me, don't you? I didn't take them."

Sidney hesitated, but Jane came to the girl's defense. "Of course we believe you, Mary. Why would you want to steal them? You would've won them anyway."

Sidney had to admit Jane was right. Mary had already won several prizes that night, and she probably would have won these prizes as well.

34

"And you were with us most of the time," Sidney added.

"But who would do this?" Mary cried out, taking the horseshoe from Jane. "Why would someone want to frame me?"

Jane shrugged and brushed her mussed hair back from her face. "I don't know."

Sidney knew, though, and she knew Jane did, too. She was just too nice to say it. Mary wasn't popular, and her snippy attitude had turned many of the riding students against her. Some of them would love to see her in trouble.

"I think it's just a mean prank," Sidney said. "Someone wants to get to you."

Mary paused and ran her finger over the edge of the shiny metal shoe. "Because I was mean to them?"

Sidney and Jane looked at each other helplessly. Fortunately, before they were forced to reply, Mrs. Fitzpatrick came in, followed by the two girls who had run off to get her.

"What's going on?" the riding instructor said. "You found the game prizes?"

Mary held the horseshoe out, and Jane handed over the gift card.

Mrs. Fitzpatrick took the prizes with a smile. "Thank goodness, girls. I'm so glad."

"But she stole them, Mrs. Fitzpatrick," the angry girl behind Mrs. Fitzpatrick argued, her hands on her hips. "She should be punished, shouldn't she?"

"Did you take these, Mary?" Mrs. Fitzpatrick looked at Mary seriously.

Mary shook her head, her eyes solemn. "No, ma'am. I have no idea how they got there."

"That's good enough for me." Mrs. Fitzpatrick shrugged her shoulders. "There's no harm done. We have them back now."

"But isn't she going to be punished?" The girl who had tattled asked, looking up at Mrs. Fitzpatrick with wide eyes.

"No, Penny. Whoever took them shouldn't have, but it is Christmas, isn't it? A time for forgiveness?"

Penny groaned and stomped away, flopping onto her bed with crossed arms. Sidney sighed with relief. Mrs. Fitzpatrick had jumped to conclusions about her in the past, just as Sidney had about Bryan when they had first met, and she had been afraid that Mrs. Fitzpatrick would assume the worst about Mary. They had all learned some hard lessons since then, though. Mrs. Fitzpatrick winked at Sidney as if reading her thoughts.

"Besides, I've assumed guilt in the past, and I was wrong. Can you prove that Mary took the prizes?" Mrs. Fitzpatrick asked Penny. "She says she didn't, and I believe her."

Penny shook her head, her brown braids flying, and glared at Mary, who looked away shyly.

"If anyone else had taken it, they would have been punished. You just let her get away with anything because her mother's dead."

Everyone gaped at the girl and Mrs. Fitzpatrick gasped audibly. "How dare you, Penny? What a horrible thing to say. That's not true in the least."

But Mary shook her head. She looked at the horseshoe in Mrs. Fitzpatrick's hand then stared right back at the girl.

"No, it is true, Mrs. Fitzpatrick. I've been mean and grumpy, and you've let me be mean because you were too nice to hurt my feelings."

"Mary-" Mrs. Fitzpatrick started.

"No, let me apologize. I won't be mean and grumpy anymore. I didn't take those." Mary gestured toward the prizes. "But my behavior has been unacceptable. My mother never would have let me act that way." Mary paused and stared right at her accuser. "I'm sorry, Penny."

Penny seemed to relax. The sneer slowly dropped from her face, and she hung her head. There was a long minute of silence, then Penny spoke, her voice trembling.

"I shouldn't have brought up your mother. I'm the one who should be sorry."

"No, I shouldn't have treated everyone so badly. Do you think you can forgive me? I promise to stop being such a Negative Nancy."

36

Penny snorted and gave Mary a small smile and a curt nod.

Mrs. Fitzpatrick looked between the girls and shook her head. "You girls are growing up. Solving your own problems. You don't even need me, do you?"

Mary reached out and took Mrs. Fitzpatrick's hand. "I do. Can I go see Sadie now?"

Mrs. Fitzpatrick bent down and wrapped her arms around Mary, giving her a quick squeeze, then she pulled her up from the mattress. "Yes, you can. In fact, I was just about to come get you anyway. I have a surprise for you."

"I don't know if I can handle any more surprises," Mary said. "Can Sidney and Jane come, too?"

Sidney looked up at her riding instructor with pleading eyes.

"Sure. But we have to be quiet." Mrs. Fitzpatrick put a finger to her lips. "We can't interrupt them."

"Interrupt who?"

"You'll see."

\*\*\*

After waiting for the three girls to wrap up again, Mrs. Fitzpatrick led the way into the barn. Sidney took a deep breath and let it out. Her breath hung in a cloud just in front of her face. Despite her gloves, her fingers felt stiff from the cold almost immediately. She flexed them, trying to stay warm, while Mrs. Fitzpatrick dug in the desk drawer for a flashlight.

"It wasn't the ideal night for this, but everything seems okay now," Mrs. Fitzpatrick said. She switched the flashlight on and gave Mary a wink. "I think you'll be really shocked."

The older woman led them to Sadie's stall by the beam of light, not bothering to turn the barn lights on, and she leaned over the top half of the stall door, looking down.

"What are you looking at?" Mary asked. "Sadie's standing up again!"

37

Sadie stood with her head hanging, munching tiredly on hay from her manger. She didn't look sweaty or agitated anymore, just exhausted.

Mrs. Fitzpatrick aimed the beam down at Sadie's feet. There, curled up in the fresh wood shavings on the stall floor, was a little horse. A foal.

Mary squealed, and the baby horse jerked its head up. Mrs. Fitzpatrick put a finger to her lips again.

"Remember. Quiet. Mama and baby need to rest."

"But I didn't know," Mary said. "Why didn't I know?"

"Your father knew, and he told me. That's why Sadie had to have all the special feeds and attention. She needed it because she was expecting a little one. Didn't you notice that she'd gotten bigger?"

"I thought she was just getting fat standing in her stall all day," Mary said with a giggle. "Where we used to live, she had a whole pasture to herself, so I thought she wasn't getting enough exercise. Why wouldn't Daddy want me to know?"

"Your father didn't want you to worry about her, and he wanted to surprise you. He knows how special she is to you."

Sidney whistled and shook her head.

"This is crazy."

She hadn't paid much attention to Sadie since she was forbidden from caring for the horse, so she hadn't noticed her growing stomach. All the strange rules made more sense now, though. Pregnant mares had to be on special diets sometimes, and Mary's father wouldn't have wanted anyone to mess that up.

Sidney poked her head over the stall beside Mary, and Jane pushed between them. They oohed and aahed over the foal together.

"It's a little boy." Mrs. Fitzpatrick gave the flashlight to Mary, who ran the light over the foal's fuzzy body. His coat was a dark brown color, and he had a small white star right in the center of his forehead.

"He's beautiful. Mom would've loved him."

Mary choked up a little bit, tears coming to her eyes, and Sadie moved over, stepping carefully around her new charge, to nuzzle Mary's hand.

"Why didn't you tell me tonight?" Mary asked her riding instructor. "I thought she was dying."

Mrs. Fitzpatrick shook her head and clenched her jaw.

"Things were looking bad there for a while. She had some problems. And one reason you didn't notice how big she'd grown is because she wasn't quite ready to have him yet. He came early."

"So she *was* in trouble?" Mary asked.

Mrs. Fitzpatrick nodded. "Oh, yes. I definitely wasn't pretending. And you need to thank Dr. Parsons. He did a great job with her, and he's not even your regular vet. He delivered the foal while we were out caroling. Then he stuck around to make sure everything would be okay with mother and baby. He didn't want you to come out and see her until he knew they would both be okay."

"Where is Dr. Parsons now?"

"He went on home to get some rest. The poor man was half-frozen."

Mary ran her hand down Sadie's forehead and tickled the whiskers on the horse's nose.

"I'll be sure to thank him personally. I almost lost you tonight, Sadie. But thanks to Dr. Parsons, I gained another horse instead. Another friend. More than one, in fact."

She turned to look at Sidney and Jane, who smiled back at her.

Sidney shivered and rubbed her gloved hands together. She could hear the wind whipping around the barn outside. The weather hadn't gotten any better. In fact, it sounded much worse.

"Sadie, your baby came right in the middle of a snowstorm," Sidney said to the horse in a scolding voice. "Probably the worst time he could've come."

"I'm glad he came while we're here, though." Jane smiled down at the foal. He stood up shakily, very shakily, on long, thin legs and walked clumsily to his mother's side. "I've never seen a newborn foal before. I didn't know they could stand up so fast!"

The girls giggled, and watched as the foal began to nurse.

"He looks like he's on stilts," Mary said.

The foal wobbled and almost fell, and the girls gasped, but he managed to keep his balance and continued suckling.

"What are you going to name him, Mary?" Sidney asked.

Mary watched him silently for a minute. "I'll have to think about it. He needs a perfect name. One that suits him."

His short, fluffy tail twitched wildly, and Sadie turned her head to nudge his rump with her nose.

"I think we should let them be now," Mrs. Fitzpatrick said, looking over the pair one last time. "They need to rest, and so do we."

The girls nodded, and they turned their backs on the sweet scene reluctantly to follow their instructor back down the barn aisle toward the warmth of their beds.

"I'll let you in on a little secret," Mrs. Fitzpatrick said at the door of the bunk room. "We're going on an early morning ride tomorrow. We can watch the sun rise over the snow."

"I wonder how much snow there'll be by tomorrow?" Jane asked her, rubbing at the goose bumps on her bare arms. They had discarded the jackets that had been thrown on over their pajamas. Sidney couldn't wait to climb back under the warm covers in the cozy bunk bed.

"I'm hoping plenty. Then I can send you all out to play while I clean up in here." She looked around the wrecked area where the party had been, and at the piles of dishes in the kitchen sink. All the food had been put away, but the smells lingered. Gingerbread. Cookies. Spices.

"Smells like Christmas in here," Sidney said, licking her lips. "Wake me up early. I'll help you clean up. If I can have the first helping of leftovers…"

Mrs. Fitzpatrick laughed and pushed Sidney gently toward the bunkroom.

"Go to sleep. I'll see you girls in the morning."

# Chapter Six

## New Beginnings

In spite of their excitement, the girls slept easily that night. Sidney had barely made it back to her warm bed before her eyes began to droop. As soon as her head hit the pillow, she was off to dreamland. She didn't wake until morning when Mrs. Sinclair leaned into the bunkroom and called out, "Good morning, girls!"

Groans and whispers filled the bunkroom as the girls stirred in their beds.

Sidney rolled over to stare at Mrs. Sinclair. "Mom, what are you doing here?"

"I came over to help Mrs. Fitzpatrick with breakfast, and with preparation for your morning activities. Your mother's here, too," she said to Jane.

Jane clambered down from the top bunk, rubbing at her bleary eyes.

"Food's on the table." Sidney's mother waited until every last one of them had gotten up before herding them out of the bunkroom and heading back to the kitchen herself.

She smiled and clapped Mary on the back as she passed her.

"I met the new baby. He's just beautiful. Congratulations."

"I think Sadie is the one who should be congratulated." Mary grinned and sniffed the air. "Gosh, this is the best sleepover I've ever been to. I've never had so much good food."

Plates filled with pancakes and bacon had already been set out for the girls, and Sidney grabbed one. The bottom of the paper plate felt hot against her hands. She poured a generous helping of maple syrup over the steaming pancakes, dipping a piece of bacon in the gooey mess before popping it into her mouth.

She chewed happily while Mrs. Abbot poured a glass of milk for her. Jane's mother had been put on beverage duty while Mrs. Sinclair went to the boys' bunkroom to wake them up, too.

Instead of fighting for a seat at one of the craft tables or at the kitchen counter, Sidney and Jane found a quiet corner and plopped right down on the floor. Sidney balanced her plate on her lap and waved for Mary to join them.

The ebony-haired girl looked better than Sidney had ever seen her. Her brown eyes shone brightly, and the smile she bestowed upon her new friends gave away just how ecstatic she felt.

"I can't wait to go out and see him again!"

"Me either!" Jane squealed. "He's so adorable."

Mary smeared butter onto her pancakes with a plastic knife.

"I really appreciate what you guys did last night. Sticking up for me."

"It was nothing. We know you didn't do it, Mary," Sidney said. And it was true. Sidney wasn't sure who had stolen the prizes and hidden them, but she felt sure Mary hadn't done it.

Bryan and Jimmy came over and sat down with the girls. After being woken up, the boys had converged on the food table and now most of the serving platters were bare. Mrs. Sinclair was busy at the kitchen sink washing dirty dishes, while Mrs. Abbot served the last of the stragglers.

"How's it going?" Bryan said sleepily. He took a large gulp of milk, and looked from one girl to the other. "You look pretty happy."

The girls exchanged a secretive glance.

"They don't know," Sidney said. "They didn't get to see last night."

42

"Know what?" Jimmy asked. His blond hair stuck out from under his cowboy hat, which looked like it had been smushed onto his head straight out of bed.

"About Mary's new horse," Jane said, elbowing Mary. "Tell them."

The boys looked expectantly at Mary, who averted her eyes shyly.

"Sadie had a foal last night," she whispered.

"A foal?" Bryan stuck a forkful of food in his mouth and chewed loudly. "What? I didn't know she was going to have a foal. I want to see."

"Close your mouth when you eat, Bryan. Gross." Jane wrinkled her nose at the boy. He stuck a tongue full of chewed food out at her in response.

"Bryan!" Sidney gasped. "Disgusting. What is Mary going to think of you?"

But Mary just chuckled and took a bite of pancake herself.

"We'll go look at him as soon as we eat. Don't worry. It's hard to offend me," she said.

Mrs. Fitzpatrick, who had been absent for breakfast, came in only a minute or so later to recruit her first group for morning activities.

"We're going riding this morning. We don't have enough horses for everyone, so we're going to go in two groups. Who would like to be in the first group?"

Sidney and her friends looked at one another.

"Let's go together," Sidney said. "We can be in the first group. It doesn't look like many are volunteering."

It was true. Many of the riding students, still sleepy and now full on pancakes and milk, had sprawled out on the floor with games or had mysteriously disappeared into the bunkrooms again. Sidney suspected that a few may have slipped back into bed to continue sleeping.

The group got up and threw away their trash, joining Mrs. Fitzpatrick by the door. Jared, Jimmy's little brother, also came over, along with a few other boys his age.

Mrs. Fitzpatrick did a quick headcount.

43

"Perfect," she said. "You guys go get dressed. I'll meet you out in the barn. The horses are already tacked up and ready to go."

***

Mrs. Fitzpatrick led them out into the covered arena to mount their horses. Sidney had gotten lucky. Mrs. Fitzpatrick had assigned her to her favorite horse in the stable. She shivered and put an arm around Jasper's fuzzy neck. His winter coat had grown out, and he looked twice as furry as he did during the summer.

Jane rode her usual mount, Misty. The gray Arabian mare looked tired and annoyed at being dragged out of her stall so early in the morning. Jane stood still, holding Misty by the bridle, and Misty lowered her head and half-closed her eyes.

"She's still in sleep mode," Jane said, jiggling the reins. Misty opened her eyes briefly then closed them again.

"Mount up!" Mrs. Fitzpatrick gave the word, holding her own mount, Jasmine, by the reins while she watched her students mount. Jasmine was Jasper's sister, and she looked similar to him in everything but size. They both had shiny black coats, white markings on their bodies, and long, slightly wavy, manes and tails. She was much smaller than Jasper, though, and she was the only lesson horse Sidney had never ridden because she was for advanced riders only.

Bryan rode Magic, an antsy chestnut Quarter Horse, and Jimmy rode his own horse, Charlie, who boarded at Blue Moon Stables. They both clambered up into the saddle. Sidney expected Magic to be his usual excitable self, but even he seemed subdued. He stood quietly, waiting for the signal to go, while Bryan adjusted his stirrups.

Sidney swung up into the saddle. She sat on Jasper and fiddled with the horse's mane while she waited for everyone else to mount. The younger students took a bit longer.

Finally, when everyone was up on their horse and set to go, Mrs. Fitzpatrick mounted Jasmine and nudged the horse's sides, steering her toward the gate. When it opened, Sidney let out a gasp. A deep bed of snow surrounded the stables.

44

She glanced at Jane, excited. "Look at it!"

The students all started talking at once. "We can make snowmen! We can build snow forts! We can make snow angels!"

Mrs. Fitzpatrick laughed. "Yes, you can. Once we get back. You can spend the morning playing in the snow. I think I even have a sled somewhere. Be careful with the horses, though. We're going to keep the ride short and sweet."

Sidney had never seen so much snow in her life, and apparently neither had Jasper.

When they exited the arena and stepped onto the wintry mix for the first time, the horse looked down at the crunchy white stuff in surprise. Sidney allowed him to lower his nose and sniff the snow.

"Take your time," Mrs. Fitzpatrick said from the front. "Go slowly and let your horses figure it out."

The horse smelled the ground carefully, then he took a large bite!

"Jasper!" Sidney guffawed. "What are you doing?!?"

The horse let the snow fall from his mouth and picked up some more, then moved the snow around with his nose, digging for the grass hidden underneath. Seeming satisfied with his experiment and with the fact that the grass was still there, he lifted his head, chunks of dirtied snow still falling from his lips, and continued walking. The other horses treated the snow just as oddly. They all wanted to taste it and play with it. Their riders' let them be curious, laughing at their antics. Being from an area where large amounts of snow are uncommon, some of the horses had probably never seen snow before that morning.

After the horses had become accustomed to walking on the snowy ground, Mrs. Fitzpatrick held up a hand. "Okay. Enough of that. Let's go through the pasture."

She had already opened the gate. No horses were out to pasture this morning. They were all either being used in the ride or snug in the barn.

The morning air felt cold, but invigorating, against Sidney's skin, and it smelled crisp and fresh. Sidney took a deep breath. The freezing air hurt her lungs, but somehow felt good at the same time.

45

"It's so beautiful," she whispered. She hadn't meant for anyone to hear, but the others nodded in agreement.

Not a footprint disturbed the perfect expanse of white covering the pasture, and the soft beds of snow, mounded over tufts of grass here and there, glinted in the light of the newly risen sun, which spilled over the trees, dappling the ground in places with dark shadows.

The horses walked through the snow slowly, leaving a path of destruction in the perfect white, like a line drawn with a pen on a blank sheet of paper. They trudged across the pasture and back again, the riders keeping silent, enjoying the quiet morning. No one was out driving. No one was busy outside, mowing grass, or blowing leaves, or doing farm work. Everyone was huddled up in their houses, or maybe even still in their beds. It was a perfect quiet. The kind of quiet that comes only with a deep snow.

\*\*\*

After the first group of riders returned to the barn, the second group went out, and Sidney and her friends went to visit with Sadie's new baby in her stall.

Mary leaned over the stall door and stroked the little brown foal's forehead. He twitched his tail playfully and nibbled at her sleeve with toothless gums.

Sadie looked much more alert than she had the night before, and she fought with her baby for attention.

"Jealous, pretty girl?" Mary rubbed her horse's neck and kissed her lightly. "Don't be. You're still my special horse."

Sadie reveled in the attention, nickering to her owner and pushing her head over the stall door.

"You're tired of being cooped up in that stall, aren't you?" Sidney reached out to touch the mare's soft nose.

The baby, angry at being ignored, nipped at his mother's shoulder and pushed his head up toward Mary's hand, which was still resting lightly on his mother's neck. When his mother didn't move out of the way and Mary made

46

no move to reach down to him, he let out a little squeal and kicked out at his mother with a tiny back hoof.

"You're going to be a handful." Bryan chuckled.

He reached out to brush a hand over the foal's short mane. He had really warmed up to Mary, and Sidney was glad to see Jimmy smiling down at the foal as well. Sidney had taken a moment to pull the boys aside and tell them what had happened the night before in the girls' bunk room. The boys had been shocked to learn about Mary's mother, and they agreed they didn't think Mary had stolen the prizes.

"Why would she hide them there and then just let you pick up her pillow?" Bryan had said, shaking his head and running a hand through his shaggy brown hair. "It doesn't make any sense."

Sidney had agreed, but they hadn't had time to discuss the matter further. Mary had returned, and they had gone to the Sadie's stall together.

"So, what's the name going to be?" Jane asked. "You've had all night to think on it."

The foal nudged Bryan's arm with his nose and nickered softly.

"He's so active," Bryan said in amazement. "He's got so much energy!"

"Not that much energy. Look at his little legs. They're shaking." Jane pulled Bryan's arm away. "I think he's tired. But he's too curious to lay down and take a nap."

The foal vied for their attention for a few more minutes then dropped into the wood shavings on the stall floor, curling his long legs under him. Mary looked at the little spitfire. The baby who had been born on an unfortunate, and very cold, night in December.

"He's a Christmas baby, so he has to have a Christmas name."

"How about Nick, after St. Nick?" Jimmy suggested.

"I like that," Mary said. She cocked her head and tried it several times. "Nick. Little Nick. Or Nicky."

"That's cute." Sidney smiled down at the foal. He flicked his ears back and forth and lowered his chin to the ground, closing his eyes.

"I don't think it's quite right, though." Mary frowned. "What do you think of Rudolph? After the reindeer?"

Sidney laughed loudly with delight. "Rudolph. I love it. He does look like a little deer, doesn't he? With his brown fuzzy coat and his little broom tail."

"And there's a sleigh right outside his stall." Bryan gestured toward the unused surprise. "These could be Santa's stables."

"Rudolph," Mary repeated quietly, staring at the sleepy foal. "I'll call him Rudy for short."

"That's just perfect." Sidney put an arm around Mary's shoulder. "I think we should let Rudy get some sleep now."

The foal's bottom lip drooped. He looked warm and comfortable on the stall floor.

"Can horses snore? He looks like he should be snoring." Jane grinned.

"Yep. He looks pretty happy," Bryan backed away from the stall, tiptoeing exaggeratedly. "Let's not wake him up. To stay out of his way, we can go out and play in the snow!"

Mary's face lit up. She put a finger to her lips. "You're right. I want to build a snowman."

"Let's build a snow fort, too," Jane whispered, "or a snow castle!"

"Nah, I want to have a snowball fight," Jimmy said. "I could beat all of you."

"Well, we could build a fort first and use it in the snowball fight," Sidney offered.

Bryan waved all their ideas away with an impatient gesture of his hand.

"I've got a better idea. We can do all those things later. First, we should go sledding! I think the sled Mom was talking about is in the house."

Everyone in the group of friends grinned. It was something they could all agree on.

"Let's go!"

48

# Chapter Seven

## The Prize Thief Revealed

The driveway turned out to be perfect for sledding. It sloped gently downhill but flattened out well before it reached the road, so there was no danger of the sledders sliding into traffic. Not that there was any traffic.

"I haven't seen a single car all morning." Sidney stood at the top of the driveway with her hands on her hips, gasping for breath. She had just taken her turn with the sled, and dragging it back up the driveway after her ride had been no easy task.

Bryan sat on the long, red sled now, revving himself with his feet so he would get a fast takeoff. He let out a whoop as he pushed off and shot down the hill.

"No one wants to drive in this," Jane agreed. "It's too slick."

Sidney heard a door slam, the door of her own house. Her father stepped out onto the front porch of the Sinclairs' house across the road. She waved and her father waved back, a coffee cup clutched in one of his gloved hands.

"It's going to be easy for us to get home, Jane. How are the other kids' parents going to come get them?" Sidney looked around at the other children, playing in the snow. Several snowmen had been built, a small fort had been constructed, and snow angels decorated the barn lot. Everyone was beginning to look cold and tired. Sidney spotted many red, runny noses and chapped faces. She rubbed at her own nose, and Jane shook her head.

49

"I don't know but I could use a hot drink," she said. "What do you think, Sid? Mary? Do you want to take a break?"

"Definitely," Mary said. "I need get out of the cold and sit down. It was a long night, and I don't think I've fully recovered."

Sidney agreed gratefully, too. She didn't want to be a party pooper, but she really needed to warm up and rest for a while, and if her mother was coming over she would like to talk to her. She still hadn't figured out why her parents were acting so strange and secretive.

"We're going in," Jane yelled to Bryan, who was trudging back up the hill, pulling the sled by its string. Jimmy was almost halfway down, about to grab the sled for his turn.

"We'll come in, too," Bryan replied, handing the sled off to his friend. "Just one more ride."

Sidney, Jane, and Mary tramped through the snow and back into the barn addition, stopping at the door to remove their boots and snow-covered clothing.

Mrs. Fitzpatrick met them in the entryway. "Hot cider? You three look like you're freezing."

"We are." Sidney unwrapped her scarf and hung it by the door. The girls discarded the rest of the their outerwear in record speed and followed their riding instructor into the kitchen.

Pouring out hot cider, she handed a mug to each girl. "It's really hot. Be careful. You might want to wait a few minutes to drink it."

Sidney gasped at the warmth of the mug in her hands and quickly set it down on the counter. While they waited on the scalding cider to cool, they chatted about the horses, the morning ride, and the snow.

"Well, how's the party been overall?" Mrs. Fitzpatrick asked finally. "Have you enjoyed yourselves?"

The girls nodded, and Sidney picked up her mug to sip the steaming liquid cautiously.

"It's been… exciting," Sidney responded. "I've never been to a party like this one."

"I know I won't forget it," Mary agreed. She blew over the top of her cider, creating ripples in the cinnamon-scented liquid.

"Well, I hope that's an endorsement." Mrs. Fitzpatrick laughed. "Despite everything that happened, I'm planning on doing it again next year."

Mrs. Sinclair came in from outside, shivering as she removed her winter coat.

"Mmmm. It smells like Christmas in here. What is that?"

Mrs. Fitzpatrick laughed again. "I think it's a mixture of the hot cider and the Christmas tree I just dragged in."

She gestured toward a small tree leaning against the wall. "It was supposed to be here before the party, but in all the chaos and with the weather, I ran out of time. It never got set up."

Jane studied the bare Christmas tree. "It's cute. It could use some decorations, though."

"Your mother went to get decorations from the house," Mrs. Fitzpatrick responded. "She's in charge of fixing it up. You know how good she is at that stuff. We have a little surprise for you guys, and your mom thought we definitely needed a decorated Christmas tree for it."

"There are too many surprises at this party," Sidney complained, but she felt a glimmer of excitement. "I can't keep track of them all."

"Speaking of surprises..." Jane nudged Sidney with her elbow and gave her a look. "Ask her."

The two girls stared at Mrs. Sinclair.

"Ask me what?" Mrs. Sinclair raised an eyebrow.

"I overheard you and Mrs. Fitzpatrick talking last night..." Sidney bit her lip and looked down at the tabletop.

"What did you hear?" Mrs. Sinclair's green eyes widened. "That was a private conversation, Sid."

"I know, Mom," Sidney said. "I'm sorry."

She paused, trying to think of something to say and just as she was about to open her mouth BAM! The door banged open and Derek burst in from outside. Sidney frowned. He had been causing trouble again that morning, picking on the smaller children who were playing in the snow. She didn't want to have to deal with him again.

He slid into the kitchen area on wet, snowy boots.

"I know who did it!" He gasped for breath and tore at the scarf around his neck. "I know who did it!"

Mrs. Sinclair stood up quickly, setting her cup down on the counter. "Know who did what? What's wrong?"

"Took the prizes," Derek gasped out. "I've found the person who stole them." He put his hands on his hips and threw his head back triumphantly. "You're never gonna guess."

Mary rolled her eyes and set her cup down as well.

"Are you going to accuse me again, Derek? I've already been blamed for it, and I didn't do it. I've already been over this."

Derek snorted derisively. "No, Mary. I don't think you did it. That was Jimmy... and lots of other people."

"What was me?" Jimmy and Bryan walked in behind Derek. "And who left the door open? There's snow getting everywhere."

Bryan closed the door behind them, shutting off the flow of cold air.

"You thought I stole the prizes," Mary said to Jimmy, staring him straight in the face.

"Only at the very beginning. Not... not anymore," Jimmy stuttered. He removed his coat and gloves, not meeting Mary's gaze. "I don't think you did it. It would be too obvious. If you took them, you wouldn't hide them in your stuff like that. Right on your bed where anyone could find them."

Derek stomped his foot, angry at all the attention being stolen away from him. "Listen up! It wasn't Mary."

They all turned to stare at Derek and he grinned with a mean gleam in his eye.

"But I know who it was." He paused, staring at Jimmy.

"Well?" Jimmy threw his hands in the air. "Are you going to tell us?"

Derek opened his mouth, savoring the moment, but before he could get it out, the door creaked open again a little head poked in. "I know what he's going to tell you, and I want to be the one to do it."

The small figure inched into the room, looking from face to face, nervously twisting his hands together in front of him.

"I took the prizes. I hid them in Mary's bed. I'm the thief."

\*\*\*

"Well, that was a surprising turn of events," Sidney said.

Derek had stomped from the room with a scathing glance at Jared, who he blamed for ruining his great revelation, and Mrs. Sinclair and Mrs. Fitzpatrick had marched off with Jared.

"Why would he do that?" Jimmy lowered his brows and slammed a fist onto the kitchen counter. "He's not the kind of kid that would steal."

"Do you really not know, Jimmy?" Jane put a hand on his shoulder. "He did it for you."

"For me?"

"You were so angry and upset when Mary was winning all the games. Don't you see how he looks up to you? How much he admires you? I think he was just trying to help you."

Sidney nodded in agreement. "He wanted to impress you, Jimmy."

Jimmy looked around at his friends. "I'm sorry, guys. I didn't mean to be such a bad loser."

He looked at Mary, who met his gaze with a smile.

"I think bad loser is a bit of an understatement," she said. "But I'll forgive you. Maybe we can do a rematch sometime?"

"Yeah, a rematch."

Jimmy put out a hand and Mary took it, shaking it gently. "Friends?"

"Friends." Mary smiled.

"Do you think Jared will be in big trouble with Mrs. Fitzpatrick?" Jimmy asked quietly, hanging his head.

Sidney gave him a quick hug. "No, but maybe you should go explain to her, and to Jared, what happened, and tell Jared that he doesn't need to you impress you. You're already impressed."

"That's true," Jimmy said. "His riding has improved so much over the last couple months. He works really hard at it. Harder than I ever did at his age."

"It's because he wants to be just like you, Jimmy."

"Well, I'll go talk to him, and to Mrs. Fitzpatrick. I'll make sure she knows this is my fault."

Jimmy walked off slowly, looking thoughtful.

"I think this is good for the both of them," Jane said, watching him go. "It'll open his eyes to how much Jared looks up to him. That kid pays attention to everything he does. He needs to be a good role model for him."

Bryan picked up an empty mug and filled it with cider. "Yeah. It annoys him being followed around all the time, though. That's one of the reasons we disappeared at the party last night. He was tired of Jared bugging him. He gets teased for it, you know, when his little brother constantly tags along."

Sidney frowned. "Boys are ridiculous. If I had a little sister, I'd want her to follow me around and look up to me."

"Yeah, right. You hate it when Derek follows you around at the stables," he said, pointing an accusing finger at Sidney.

"That's different."

"No, it isn't." Bryan sipped from his cup and gagged. "This is blazing hot."

He set the cup back down on the counter.

"Derek bothers you all the time because he's bored and he doesn't get any attention," he said. "That's why he's such a troublemaker, too."

Jane stared at Bryan, realization dawning on her face. "I think you're right."

54

"You don't have to sound so surprised." Bryan looked offended. "I know what I'm talking about."

Sidney crossed her arms and stared at the table, frowning. "I never thought of it that way. I guess I am pretty mean to Derek sometimes when he really just wants to help or talk to me."

Mary stood up.

"I think we should all pay attention to people more," she said, "and not take them for granted. I know that better than anyone, and I've been terrible about it. I'm going to try harder from now on, though"

Sidney looked up at her new friend. "You're right, Mary. I'll make more of an effort with Derek."

"And I promise to be nicer," Mary responded. "Not just with Derek, but with everyone. Maybe then I won't be the most hated girl at the stables."

A smile tugged at the corners of her mouth.

"But I'll still be the best at games. Just wait until we try them on horseback. I'll have you all beat."

"Wanna bet?" Sidney grinned. She always enjoyed a little friendly competition.

***

In the end, Jared didn't get into trouble for taking the prizes. He apologized to everyone, and Mrs. Fitzpatrick proposed that the games continue. And they did, with Mary coming out the clear winner.

When the games had finished, Mrs. Fitzpatrick handed Mary the golden horseshoe and the gift card with a smile.

"The horseshoe may not be very useful, but you can use the gift card to buy Rudy a few things."

"Thanks, Mrs. Fitzpatrick, but I'm not going to keep the gift card. The horseshoe is what really matters to me, and I have a feeling there will be some presents under the tree for Rudy. Dad mentioned as much when I talked to him on the phone a little while ago."

She held the horseshoe to her chest, and looked up at her riding instructor with shining eyes. "I'll treasure this forever. It's special."

"Then what are you going to do with the gift card?" Mrs. Fitzpatrick asked, looking pleased.

"I'd like to give it to Sidney."

Sidney stared at her friend, surprised. "What?"

Mary forced the card into her hands.

"Just take it, Sid. You were so great last night, calling the vet and waiting with me. And you and Jane both stood up for me and believed me when Penny accused me." She smiled a shy smile. "I want you to have it."

Sidney took the card and held onto it. "Thanks, Mary."

"You deserve it, Sidney. I just wish I had something for all of you." She looked at Jane, Bryan, and Jimmy. "I feel like you're all my friends now."

The little group smiled back at her, and Mrs. Fitzpatrick held up her hand.

"Well, it's time for my final Christmas party surprise. I've just gotten word that some parents are battling their way through the snow to come pick you up." Her eyes roved over the students gathered around her. "I'll have to make this fast."

She turned toward the door and put her hand up beside her mouth. "Santa? Santa Claus?"

"Santa?" Jane giggled, turning to Sidney. "Really?"

"What? You didn't think Santa would make an appearance at a Christmas party?" Mrs. Fitzpatrick replied, and the door opened, revealing a very plump Santa Claus with a huge red satchel thrown over his shoulder.

"Ho! Ho! Ho!" Santa cried, taking long strides into the room. "I've got some presents for you!"

Some of the kids murmured to one another and pointed, and some just stared. No one had expected Santa Claus to show up. The large, bearded man went from one student to the next handing out presents. The packages were all wrapped with different colored Christmas paper and were varying sizes and lengths.

"Who got these presents for us?" Derek asked suspiciously when he was handed his.

"Why I did, of course." Santa laughed a deep, hearty laugh, slapping his knee.

Derek ripped the paper off his gift. "No way!"

"What is it?" Mrs. Fitzpatrick beamed.

"New riding boots! They're in my size, too."

"I got a new helmet!" Another girl cried from across the room.

Santa bent down on one knee in front of Sidney and handed her a gift. The silver wrapping paper glittered in the light. She looked into Santa's eyes. That teasing gleam looked familiar. Could it be?

"Thanks, Santa."

She could see his smile through his white beard. "You're welcome, Sidney Sinclair."

"How did you know my name?" Sidney narrowed her brown eyes and searched the face for clues, but most of it was covered up with a big beard. He also had on glasses, and his fuzzy white and red hat was pulled down low over his forehead.

"I know a lot of things. I know this isn't your last Christmas surprise. You'll have a big one on Christmas morning."

She wanted to ask more, but she saw Mrs. Fitzpatrick watching her, waiting on her to open the gift. Mrs. Fitzpatrick waved a hand at her, gesturing for her to hurry. She looked too excited for Sidney to ignore her, and when Sidney looked back, Santa had moved on to the next child.

Sidney peeled the wrapping paper off her package to reveal a plain white box, the kind that usually holds clothes. She lifted the lid off. Nestled inside was a brand new pair of breeches.

"These are kind that professional riders wear," Sidney said in awe.

Mrs. Fitzpatrick sidled over. "Do you like them?"

Sidney lifted them out of the box and held them up. "I love them! I wasn't expecting anything."

57

"Well, it's been a good year. And I wanted to reward my students for their hard work and dedication. The parents helped out, too."

"Can I go try them on?" Sidney asked. "I can't wait to wear them!"

"Sure, but be careful. You'll need to keep them in good shape for when you start showing this summer."

Mrs. Fitzpatrick winked and walked off, leaving Sidney gaping behind her.

"Showing?" Jane squealed and grabbed Sidney's hand.

"Look what I got!" She held out a pretty silver necklace decorated with little horseshoes.

"That's beautiful, Jane."

Squeals and excited yells were going up all the around the room, but all Sidney could hear were Mrs. Fitzpatrick's last words.

When you start showing this summer....

# Chapter Eight

## The Final Surprise

The party finally ended just after noon when the last parent struggled up the snowy driveway to pick up the last child, which just happened to be Derek, the little troublemaker.

Jimmy and Jared had gone home about an hour before, and Mary's father had arrived only moments after their departure. The party goers had slowly dwindled until only Bryan, Sidney, Jane, and Derek were left.

Sidney walked out with the Derek to meet his mother, and she smiled and waved as the boy climbed into his parent's mini-van.

"See you at lessons next week," Sidney said. "I may need your help with a few things."

Derek beamed back at her and nodded.

"Awesome."

He slammed the car door and Sidney watched the van crawl carefully back down the driveway, the tires crunching on the snow.

She paused, surveying the messy barnyard. The snow had been disturbed all around the barn. The noon sun had begun to melt the snow, and the snowmen looked a little droopy. A carrot nose had fallen into the snow at Sidney's feet, and she picked it up.

"A carrot for Rudolph," she said to herself quietly, and she went back into the barn.

The horses munched on their hay, content in the comfort of their stalls. Sidney leaned over Sadie's stall door.

"How are you doing, girl?" she asked, rubbing the horse's neck. "Feeling better?"

She stuck the carrot out, holding it flat on her palm, and Sadie picked it up, crunching it loudly with her teeth. Orange-colored juice ran from her mouth and dripped onto the wood shavings on the floor.

Rudy watched with interest, nudging at his mother's chest.

"You can't eat carrots just yet, buddy." Sidney reached out and touched the foal's fuzzy back. The baby horse flinched and gazed up at her, annoyed.

"You'll like it one day. Look at your mom. She loves to be petted."

The foal flicked his brown ears back and forth then turned his back on her. *Arrogant little thing.* She giggled at the haughty look in his bright brown eyes.

"Well, I better get inside and start cleaning with the rest of them," Sidney said to the horses. Rudy ignored her, but Sadie pointed an ear toward Sidney, listening. *Horses always listen,* Sidney thought, and she pushed away from the stall.

Sidney's and Jane's mothers almost had the party area spic and span again, though, and they didn't need much help.

"You two have been amazing," Mrs. Fitzpatrick said, looking from Mrs. Sinclair to Mrs. Abbot. "I have a little something for you to thank you."

The two women glanced at one another, surprised.

"I think you've given out plenty of gifts already." Mrs. Sinclair laughed. "Even I wasn't expecting Santa Claus."

"Well, just two more." Mrs. Fitzpatrick went to the utility closet and pulled out a box, opening it up. "Shirt size?" She held out an armful of baby blue T-shirts.

Mrs. Sinclair grabbed one and unfolded it. "A small. Perfect. And it's just beautiful." Large black letters spelled out Blue Moon Stables across the front of a shirt, and a full moon hovered just behind the words.

Mrs. Abbot picked out one of the shirts, too, and slipped it over her head right over the top of her Christmas sweater.

"Cool. I want one, Mom," Bryan said.

He threw down the rag he had been using to wipe down the tables and dug through the box of T-shirts until he came across one his size.

He discarded his jacket and put the shirt on, modeling it for everyone.

Sashaying down the hallway, he did a small spin at the end then walked back like he was on a catwalk.

Jane snorted, trying to hold her laughter in. "You're ridiculous, Bryan."

Mrs. Fitzpatrick chuckled, too.

"The shirts did turn out well, though," she said. "In fact, this entire venture has turned out better than I ever could have expected. My dream of owning stables has come true. Not many people can say that, can they? That they're living their dream?"

"No, they can't. And you put on a great party, Mrs. Fitzpatrick," Sidney said, seeing the joy in everyone's eyes. "Everyone had a great time. I think it was success."

"Thank you, Sidney. It was rocky there for a while but the Christmas spirit always comes through in the end, doesn't it?"

Sidney met her instructor's glowing eyes and grinned.

"Yes, it does."

\*\*\*

"Wake up, Sidney!" Sidney's eyes flew open. The loud knock on her bedroom door repeated. "It's Christmas morning!"

Sidney sat up groggily. "I'm coming. Don't start without me!"

"I'll make the hot chocolate and cinnamon rolls. Get dressed and come down stairs," her mother said from the other side of the door.

Sidney didn't respond. She just rolled out of her rumpled bed and staggered to her dresser drawers, pulling out a shirt and a pair of jeans.

"Shower?" Sidney said aloud to herself then shook her head. A shower could wait until later. After presents.

She tugged off her nightgown and replaced it with real clothes, brushed her hair and teeth quickly, and stormed down the stairs. By that time, she had fully awakened, and she could smell the cinnamon rolls baking in the kitchen. Licking her lips, she made her way toward the smell, avoiding looking at the Christmas tree. She wanted to wait until she was ready to rip the presents open to look at the gloriousness of the Christmas tree on Christmas morning. It was always a vision she savored.

Her mother stood in front of the stove, spatula in hand, her ginger-colored hair mussed and unbrushed. Her mother acted more like a child on Christmas morning than Sidney did. She loved to be the first person up, and she usually dragged everyone out of bed earlier than they would've liked so they could all open presents. This morning she seemed extra eager.

"Your dad should be down any minute." Mrs. Sinclair poured out a cup of hot chocolate for her daughter, adding a handful of oversized marshmallows. "Are you excited?"

She handed Sidney the warm cup and turned back to the stove, not waiting for an answer. How could anyone not be excited on Christmas morning? She pulled out the tray of cinnamon rolls and set them out to cool on the cooling rack with the spatula.

"I smell something delicious!" Sidney's father said, walking in from the living room. He hooked a thumb back toward the tree. "And did you see all those presents? Someone must have been good this year."

He gave Sidney a swift peck on the cheek as he passed. "Ready to open them up?"

Sidney nodded. "Can we start now?" Excitement bubbled up in her stomach, and she took a small sip of her hot chocolate.

"Sure. Just let me grab one of these delicious cinnamon rolls." Her father scooped up an un-iced cinnamon roll and popped it into his mouth.

"Oh, that's hot!" He chewed quickly and swallowed.

"Of course it is! It just came out of the oven. I haven't even put the icing on them yet." Sidney's mother put her hands on her hips.

"Now it's your job." She forced the icing bag into Mr. Sinclair's hands.

After Mr. Sinclair finished icing the cinnamon rolls, Mrs. Sinclair helped him plate them up and fixed hot chocolates for both of them.

"Now we're ready," he said, leading the way into the living room, carefully balancing the plate of cinnamon rolls in one hand while holding his hot cup of cocoa in the other.

Sidney followed, stopping by the sofa to stare at the tree. Multi-colored presents were scattered about under the trees branches. The lights on the tree twinkled and gleamed, reflecting off the shiny wrapping paper on the gifts. Ribbons and bows decorated every package. It looked just perfect. Like it did every year.

Sidney's father gestured toward the tree. "Dig in."

Not all the presents were for Sidney, so she sorted out her gifts from the others and handed the other gifts out first. She liked to play Santa.

"From Dad, to Mom," she read off, handing the large box to her mother.

Her mother smiled and looked over at Mr. Sinclair affectionately. "Is this what I think it is?"

He shrugged. "You'll have to open it to find out."

Mrs. Sinclair tore the wrapping paper off the present and pulled open the box.

"It is!" She held up a pretty red dress, one she had been admiring for weeks in the window of a local clothing store.

"It's beautiful, Mom! You can wear that to the New Year's Eve party."

Mr. and Mrs. Sinclair always attended a New Year's Eve party at a neighbor's house while Sidney slept over with Jane. Mrs. Sinclair went over to give her husband a kiss and took a seat beside on him on the couch.

"Now you open one of yours, Sid," Mrs. Sinclair said, folding the dress back up and placing it carefully back into the box.

Sidney plowed through her presents. She got a lot of horse stuff and some new clothes and books. Her father got a new watch from Mrs. Sinclair. When her parents opened her present to the both of them, she smiled. She had gotten them a framed family photo. Even Herbert, the Sinclairs' hateful cat, was in the photo.

"I think everyone's had a pretty good Christmas," Mr. Sinclair said, stretching out on the couch.

Sidney sat on the floor amid piles of wrapping paper and discarded bows.

"Well, I guess Christmas is over," Mrs. Sinclair said, gathering the empty hot chocolate cups to take to the kitchen.

"Thanks, Mom. Thanks, Dad. I love all my gifts. You're the best!"

Sidney looked around at her Christmas haul with a smile. She couldn't have asked for more. She was a little confused, though. What was her mom talking about with Mrs. Fitzpatrick during their "private conversation"? Which present could have prompted such a strange reaction?

"What's that noise?" Mr. Sinclair cocked his head to the side and put a hand to his ear.

"What noise?" Sidney looked up curiously. "I don't hear anything."

"Listen." Mr. Sinclair held up a finger.

Sidney's parents exchanged secretive glances. "What's going on?"

"Bells?" Sidney knitted her brows together. "I hear bells."

Mr. Sinclair yawned and clambered up off the couch. "Maybe we should go outside and see what it is."

"Maybe," Mrs. Sinclair agreed. She set the cups back down on the side table.

The three walked outside, the bells getting louder all the time.

"No!" Sidney said loudly when she saw it. "I don't believe it. The sleigh!"

Sidney blinked at the sight. It was the sleigh Mrs. Fitzpatrick had rented for the party. And it was coming up the driveway. With Santa Claus driving it! And a horse tied to the back!

The sleigh came to a stop right in front of the Sinclairs' front porch. The family stood gathered on the steps.

"Ho! Ho! Ho!" Santa leapt down, jiggling a large, bumpy belly that looked like it had probably been fashioned from a pillow.

"Mrs. Fitzpatrick?" Sidney laughed. "Is that you?"

Mrs. Fitzpatrick pulled the beard down.

"Sorry. I couldn't resist the costume." She crinkled her eyes at Sidney. "Are you surprised?"

"Very. What is this?"

Sidney looked up at her parents. They looked back down at her, excited, and Sidney's father squeezed her shoulder.

"You deserve this, Sid." Her mother gestured toward the horse tied to the back of the sleigh. The horse pricked his ears forward and looked at her curiously with expressive brown eyes.

"This is Arthur. Your new horse." Mrs. Fitzpatrick untied him and led him over to the steps. "Come meet him."

Sidney stood frozen, stock still, staring at the big bay. He was too beautiful to be true. His black mane and tail had been braided with green and red ribbon, and his dark brown coat had been groomed until it shone. Someone had put a lot of work into this horse. "He's mine?"

She looked up at her parents again, and they both nodded.

"You've been so responsible, and you obviously love riding. You've stuck with it, and we want to reward that. Arthur is a great horse. I think you'll get along together wonderfully."

Mrs. Sinclair reached out to touch the white star on the bay horse's forehead.

"That's why I couldn't go to the party. I had to go look at Arthur," Mr. Sinclair said to Sidney. "I'm sorry about missing it, but I was afraid they'd sell him if I waited."

"I'm glad you didn't," Sidney said, still in disbelief.

Mrs. Fitzpatrick pushed the lead rope into Sidney's hands. "He's seven years old. He's a Quarter Horse and Arabian mix. That's called a Quarab. He's been shown before, and I think he'll be a great partner for you."

Mrs. Fitzpatrick's words from the party came back to Sidney. *When you start showing this summer.* So this had been the plan.

"I overheard you talking about a surprise at the party. You were talking about Arthur."

Mrs. Sinclair nodded. "I'm just glad you didn't overhear enough to ruin it." She smiled down at her daughter. "You seem a little shocked. Do you like him?"

Sidney closed her eyes for a moment and opened them again, staring at her new horse.

"Of course I do. I just feel like I'm dreaming. I think I'm about to wake up."

The adults laughed, and Sidney reached out a hand to rub Arthur's neck.

"I'll have to get to know him. He's a stranger," Sidney said.

"You'll have plenty of time for that. Your parents are boarding him at Blue Moon. You can just walk across the road and ride him anytime you want." Mrs. Fitzpatrick patted Sidney on the shoulder. "In fact, why don't you come ride him this afternoon? I'm sure Bryan would love to go riding with you. You could even invite Jane."

Sidney threw her arms around her riding instructor. "You're the best, Mrs. Fitzpatrick. Thank you, thank you, thank you."

Mrs. Fitzpatrick blushed, but she looked very pleased. Sidney turned to her parents, who beamed at her with shining eyes.

"I can't thank you enough." She gave them hugs as well, squeezing them close to her. "You're the best parents in the world."

Finally, she turned to Arthur. She wrapped her arms around his neck and buried her face in his mane.

"This has been the best Christmas ever," she whispered to the horse. "I'll take very good care of you. I love you already." Arthur nickered and nudged Sidney's shoulder with his velvety nose.

Mrs. Fitzpatrick turned to Sidney's parents and grinned.

"I think we're witnessing the beginning of a beautiful friendship."


## THE END

## About The Author

Kathryn B. Butler grew up in a small town in Tennessee. Kathryn began horseback riding at the age of seven and started writing at about the same time. Horses have influenced her writing from a young age and are often featured in her stories. Kathryn has a degree in journalism, but enjoys writing fiction best.

She loves to hear from young readers, so don't hesitate to contact her at kathrynbbutler@gmail.com.

If you enjoyed this Sidney Sinclair adventure, you may want to check out The Mystery at Blue Moon Stables (Sidney Sinclair Adventure #1) and The Riding Camp Riddle (Sidney Sinclair Adventure #2).

Made in the USA
Lexington, KY
13 April 2019